Can Julie Do Karate?

Charlie Cashman let out a hoot of laughter. "Julie's so short, I bet she'll just have to watch the rest of us doing karate in gym."

Frowning, Julie stepped forward. She only came up to Charlie's chin. "I can learn karate, and nobody can stop me."

"Yeah," Jessica said loudly. "I bet she'll be the best in the whole class."

Some of the boys began to laugh, and Julie looked back at Jessica with a startled expression.

"Why did you say that?" Julie whispered.

"Sorry," Jessica whispered back. "But they were really bugging me. And I bet you will be the best."

"You think I could?" Julie asked, her face lighting up.

"You will, you'll see," Jessica said. "You'll be better than all those boys, and then they'll have to stop showing off once and for all."

Bantam Books in the SWEET VALLEY KIDS series

SWEET VALLEY KIDS

JULIE
THE
KARATE KID

Written by
Molly Mia Stewart

Created by
FRANCINE PASCAL

Illustrated by
Ying-Hwa Hu

BANTAM BOOKS
NEW YORK • TORONTO • LONDON • SYDNEY • AUCKLAND

RL 2, 005-008

JULIE THE KARATE KID

A Bantam Book / September 1994

Sweet Valley High® and Sweet Valley Kids are
trademarks of Francine Pascal

Conceived by Francine Pascal

Produced by Daniel Weiss Associates, Inc.
33 West 17th Street
New York, NY 10011

Cover art by Susan Tang

ISBN: 0-553-48103-7

Published simultaneously in the United States and Canada

Bantam Books are published by Bantam Books, a division of Bantam
Doubleday Dell Publishing Group, Inc. Its trademark, consisting of the
words "Bantam Books" and the portrayal of a rooster, is Registered in U.S.
Patent and Trademark Office and in other countries. Marca Registrada.
Bantam Books, 1540 Broadway, New York, New York 10036.

PRINTED IN THE UNITED STATES OF AMERICA

CWO   0 9 8 7 6 5 4 3 2 1

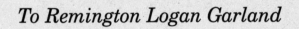

To Remington Logan Garland

CHAPTER 1

Boys Against Girls

Elizabeth Wakefield skipped to the bus stop on Monday morning. "We start karate in gym class today," she reminded her twin sister, Jessica. "It's going to be so much fun!"

Jessica made a chopping motion at a branch as they passed a leafy bush. "Take that!"

They both laughed at the same time and in the same way. Elizabeth and Jessica did many things the same way, because they were identical twins. That meant that they looked exactly alike from the tops of their heads to the ends of their toes. Both girls had long blond hair with bangs and blue-green eyes. Even their voices sounded the same. Sometimes they wore matching outfits to school. When they did that, even their friends in Mrs. Otis's second-grade class had trouble telling Elizabeth and Jessica apart.

Being twins meant Jessica and Elizabeth were exactly alike on the outside, but inside, each girl had her own special personality. Elizabeth liked playing outdoors and making up adventures in the backyard. Jessica preferred to play with her dollhouse—she thought the backyard was too messy. Elizabeth's favorite color was green and her favorite thing to do was read. Jessica liked the color pink best, and she never wanted to read—she liked talking to her friends better. Elizabeth did her homework on time, and Jessica always waited until the last minute.

But being different didn't stop the twins from being best friends. They shared everything. They shared a bedroom, they shared clothes, they even shared gum sometimes! According to Elizabeth and Jessica, having a twin sister was the most wonderful thing in the world.

"You sure got that bush," Elizabeth teased as they reached the bus stop.

Jessica took a bow. "I'm the karate champion of the world," she announced.

Behind them two boys began to laugh. Elizabeth and Jessica turned around to see their older brother, Steven, walking with Todd Wilkins, a boy from their class at Sweet Valley Elementary. Steven and Todd were both laughing.

"What's so funny?" Elizabeth asked.

Steven made a face and pointed at Jessica. "Watch out, Bruce Lee and Jean-

Claude Van Damme! My sister the karate champion is coming after you! They'll be terrified."

Todd made a karate kick in the air. "Hi-ya!" he yelled.

"The mighty ninja warrior!" Steven shouted as he made a make-believe spear jab at Todd. Todd grabbed his stomach and let out a groan.

Elizabeth and Jessica looked at each other and shook their heads. "Maybe I'm not a karate champion," Jessica said. "But you don't know anything about it, either, except what you've seen on TV."

"I do so," Todd bragged. "Ever since Mr. Cutler said we'd have a whole week of karate, Kisho has been teaching us all kinds of stuff."

"Kisho?" Elizabeth asked in surprise. "Just because his grandpa is from Japan

4

doesn't mean he knows any more karate than you do."

"That's right," Jessica said. "I bet Kisho has never even tried karate."

Some of the other kids at the bus stop gathered around. "Is the second grade doing the karate unit?" asked a third-grader named Crystal Burton.

"Yes," Elizabeth said. "Did you do it last year?"

Crystal nodded. "It was fun."

"I bet she was scared," Todd said in a loud whisper. Some of the other boys laughed.

Crystal stared at Todd. "I was not, you little shrimp," she said in her most grown-up voice.

"Girls are always afraid they'll get punched or kicked," Todd said. He flipped a quarter off his thumb and acted cool.

Elizabeth and Jessica looked at each

other. Elizabeth knew Jessica was thinking exactly what she was thinking.

"I bet the girls in our class are going to be excellent at karate," Jessica said, catching Todd's quarter just as he flipped it again. She smiled. "Just you wait."

CHAPTER 2

Kisho Shows Off

Jessica put her books on her desk in Mrs. Otis's classroom. Some of the girls were standing around the hamster cages, and most of the boys were crowded around Kisho Murasaki. He was telling them about a karate match he had seen on TV, and demonstrating all the punches and kicks as he talked. Since he had stayed back one grade, he was taller than almost all the other boys who surrounded him to listen.

"You have to call the karate teacher *sensei*," Kisho was saying. "That's Japanese for 'teacher.'"

"Look at Kisho showing off," Jessica said as she joined her friends by the hamsters.

"I can't stand it when someone acts so know-it-all," Lila Fowler said in a grumpy voice. "I bet he's making it all up, anyway."

"I wish we didn't have to do karate at all," Ellen Riteman said glumly. "My mother spent ten minutes getting this braid just right in my hair, and I don't want it messed up."

It was Julie Porter's turn to feed the class pets, and she was filling their dishes with nuts and sunflower seeds. "I'm really excited about learning karate," she said as she carefully opened Thumbelina's cage door.

Jessica was surprised. Julie was in modern-dance class with the twins. She was very athletic and graceful, but she was also the smallest girl in class—so small she almost looked like a first-grader.

9

"Aren't you afraid you'll get squashed?" Jessica asked.

Julie shook her head. "I think it looks like fun. I always wanted to try it. I even went to a karate tournament once, just to watch."

"Kisho only saw it on TV," Lila said with a giggle. "You should tell him you've been to a real live karate match. Then he'll have to stop bragging."

"Did you ask your parents if you could have lessons?" Amy Sutton asked, sitting on a desk and swinging her legs.

"They wanted me to be really sure before they sign me up," Julie explained. "They knew I'd have a chance to try it out in gym. Now I'll get to find out if I'm any good at karate."

"You?" asked a startled voice.

The girls turned. Ken Matthews was squashing his lunch bag into his overstuffed desk. He looked at Julie and grinned, showing a gap in his teeth.

"You're too small," he said with a laugh. "You have to be big, like Kisho, if you want to be any good at karate."

Jessica put her hands on her hips. "Who says?"

Ken looked over his shoulder at the other boys. "Isn't Julie too small for karate?" he asked them.

Charlie Cashman let out a hoot of laughter. "Julie? She's so short, I bet she'll just have to watch the rest of us doing karate in gym."

Frowning, Julie stepped forward. She only came up to Charlie's chin. "I can learn karate, and nobody can stop me. You don't have to be big at all."

"Yeah," Jessica said loudly. "I bet she'll be the best in the whole class."

Some of the boys began to laugh, and

11

Julie looked back at Jessica with a startled expression.

"Why did you say that?" Julie whispered.

"Sorry," Jessica whispered back. "But they were really bugging me."

"Maybe Julie will be the best," Elizabeth said with a smile. "You think I could?" Julie asked, her face lighting up.

"Sure," Elizabeth said. "I've seen you in dance class. You're very athletic."

Jessica snapped her fingers. "Yeah! And what's that word . . . coordinated! You never trip or mess up or anything."

The other girls were all nodding. Julie was smiling wider and wider. "I bet I will learn fast," she said shyly.

"You will, you'll see," Jessica said. "You'll be better than all those boys, and then they'll have to stop showing off once and for all."

CHAPTER 3

The Karate Lesson

The gymnasium echoed loudly as Mrs. Otis's class filed in for gym. The gym teacher, Mr. Cutler, stood checking attendance on his clipboard.

"Settle down, people!" he called. "Choose a buddy and sit on the floor, please!"

Instantly, Elizabeth took Jessica's hand. They were always buddies. As they sat down, Elizabeth looked to see who Julie's buddy was. Julie was sitting with Lois Waller.

Suddenly the gym door opened and a slim, black-haired Japanese man walked in. A hush fell over the group as the man crossed the floor on bare feet. He was dressed in white pants and a loose white jacket tied with a black sash.

"Wow," Jessica whispered. "A real karate master."

The man stopped in front of Mr. Cutler and bowed. "I am Mr. Ogata," he said to the children.

Mr. Cutler bowed in return. "Good morning, *sensei*. Welcome to our class."

Mr. Ogata turned and bowed solemnly to the class. The kids all looked at him in surprise. Then Elizabeth jumped up, and so did Julie and Kisho. One by one, all the students stood up and bowed. Some of the boys giggled. Mr. Cutler left the gym.

"Does anyone here already know karate?" Mr. Ogata asked in a quiet voice.

"Sure," Kisho said, stepping forward.

15

He looked back at Charlie and Ken with a grin. "I can kick."

Mr. Ogata nodded. "Would you like to demonstrate?"

Kisho straightened his back proudly. "Sure." He took a running head start across the floor and then jumped up with a yell as he kicked. Some of the boys cheered.

"How was that?" Kisho asked, panting.

"You can run very fast," Mr. Ogata replied.

Jessica leaned close to Elizabeth. "That's a polite way of saying it was no good!" she whispered.

"I know," Elizabeth replied. She smiled at Julie when Mr. Ogata asked for more volunteers.

Julie was usually shy, but she stood up and faced the karate master with a smile. "I know something."

"Please show us," Mr. Ogata said.

Julie stood with her feet wide apart and her knees slightly bent. Then she raised her fists in front of her. She looked as though nothing could knock her over.

Mr. Ogata bowed to Julie. "Very good stance. Where did you learn that?"

"From watching karate matches," Julie said. Her cheeks turned pink as she sat back down beside Lois.

"That wasn't much," Todd whispered. He and Ken were sitting behind Elizabeth and Jessica.

Elizabeth looked back at him. "It was correct, and you didn't know it," she pointed out.

"Karate is not a game," Mr. Ogata said in his quiet voice. "It is a discipline. With practice you can train your body to re-spond when you are attacked. If you are disciplined, even a small person can overcome a powerful enemy," he said, smiling at Julie.

Elizabeth felt very serious as she listened to the *sensei*. He made karate sound important and grown-up.

"The most important thing I want to teach you is that you must not fight," Mr. Ogata continued.

Charlie laughed out loud. "If we're not supposed to fight, why bother learning karate?"

Mr. Ogata turned to face Charlie. "We learn karate to defend ourselves, not to attack others. The greatest karate masters avoid fighting, because they know that someone will be hurt in a fight."

"That's not the way it is in the movies," Todd spoke up.

Mr. Ogata laughed. "The movies do not show the true meaning of karate," he said. "With discipline we learn never to fight from anger. With practice we learn to turn the anger of another back on him."

Elizabeth heard the gymnasium door open. Mr. Cutler came back in, wearing a karate uniform. He walked to Mr. Ogata and bowed.

"Are you going to fight?" Ellen asked.

"We are going to demonstrate," Mr. Ogata said.

Elizabeth looked at Jessica. "This is exciting!" she whispered.

The group fell silent as Mr. Cutler and Mr. Ogata faced off. Elizabeth noticed that they both stood in the same way that Julie had. Then the two men suddenly burst into movement—punching, kicking, turning, and rolling. They used their hands and arms to block the punches and kicks. Mr. Ogata was able to knock Mr. Cutler off balance in the middle of a turn.

In a flash Mr. Cutler was on his back, and Mr. Ogata had his hand one inch away from Mr. Cutler's throat. The whole demonstration had lasted less than a minute.

There was a hush, and then the kids began to clap and cheer. "That was so cool!" Todd yelled.

The two men stood up and bowed to each other.

"I can't wait to try it!" Elizabeth said.

"Now it is time for you to begin," Mr. Ogata said to the class.

Everyone stood up with his or her buddies, waiting eagerly. The *sensei* showed them how to stand correctly and taught them two ways to block.

"Right arm up, muscle of your forearm toward the ceiling! Left elbow comes back with your fist at your waist. Then switch arms quickly."

Mr. Ogata paced back and forth, watch-

ing the pairs of buddies. He stopped in front of Julie. "Now your arm is up," he said. "Swing it down and out, with your palm facing behind you. This will block a kick and turn it away from you."

Elizabeth and Jessica faced each other, practicing the block. Elizabeth concentrated hard on doing exactly what the teacher said. She was actually doing karate!

She looked over at Julie and smiled. No wonder Julie had wanted to learn karate. Now Elizabeth wanted to learn it as much as Julie did!

CHAPTER 4

Jessica's Baby

Jessica sat at the dinner table that night and gulped down a whole glass of milk. "Gym was so cool today," she announced as she wiped her mouth with a napkin.

"We started karate," Elizabeth added.

Mr. Wakefield began serving macaroni and cheese. "Karate? That sounds pretty exciting."

"It is," Jessica agreed. "The teacher is just like someone from a movie." She stood next to her chair and made a slow bow, just the way Mr. Ogata had taught them.

"I thought girls were supposed to curtsy," Steven said with a grin.

"That's not funny," Elizabeth said. She looked at their mother. "A lot of the boys were acting really dumb all day, pretending to be ninjas and stuff like that. But Mr. Ogata said that real karate takes control and pratice and respect. I'm going to practice the real moves, not the *fake* ones," she said, making a face at Steven.

Mrs. Wakefield laughed. "Look out, Steven. When Liz takes something seriously, she outshines everyone."

"You know who else takes it seriously?" Jessica asked. "Julie Porter. She's really good at it."

"She's in your dance class, isn't she?" Mrs. Wakefield asked. "She's very good at dance, too."

"And you could tell Mr. Ogata thought she was good," Elizabeth said. "I bet

24

she'll be the best in the class."

Steven rolled his eyes. "Oh, sure. A girl is really going to be the best fighter."

"Don't be too confident, Steven," Mr. Wakefield said. "You might end up looking pretty foolish if Liz is correct."

Jessica speared a green bean with her fork and gave her brother a haughty stare. "Boys are so dumb. They think all girls can do is easy stuff like taking care of babies."

Mrs. Wakefield choked on her food and began to cough. "Easy?" she gasped. "Taking care of babies is easy?"

"Sure," Jessica said with a shrug. "All they do is sleep and eat and lie around."

"Is that right?" Mrs. Wakefield put down her fork and pushed her chair away from the dinner table. "I'll be right back."

There was a silence around the table as Mrs. Wakefield disappeared into the kitchen.

25

Jessica looked at Elizabeth and Steven and shrugged. Mr. Wakefield began to chuckle.

"I think you just made a mistake, Jess," he said.

"What did I say?" Jessica asked in surprise. She could hear her mother opening drawers and cabinets in the kitchen. There was a muffled thump, and a clatter, and then footsteps returning.

Jessica watched in confusion as her mother came back to the dining room carrying a one-gallon plastic bag filled with dried beans. Mrs. Wakefield placed the bag on the table next to Jessica. The bag was reinforced with masking tape, and written on the tape in Magic Marker were the words: "Jessica's Baby."

"What's this?" Jessica asked, her eyes wide.

Elizabeth began to giggle. "You really asked for it."

"What?" Jessica asked again. "I don't get it."

Mrs. Wakefield returned to her seat and picked up her fork. "That's a baby. If you can take care of it until Friday, I'll treat you all to a trip to the water-slide park."

Jessica let out a startled laugh. "That's all?" She looked at Elizabeth and smiled. "Easy-peasy."

"But," Mrs. Wakefield continued, "if you drop it, or lose it, or leave it behind when you go to school, you'll have to wash my car."

Steven began to laugh. "Jessie's widdle baby," he teased.

Jessica laughed, too. "I bet you think I can't do it," she said. "But it'll be easy."

Mr. Wakefield tapped the "baby" with one finger. "Why not pick it up and see how much it weighs?"

"Sure, no problem." Jessica lifted the

bag full of beans. "It's not heavy at all."

"Wait until you've been carrying it for a week," Mrs. Wakefield said.

"I just don't think it'll be very hard," Jessica said airily. "I guess I'll pick out what bathing suit I want to wear to the water-slide park."

Mr. Wakefield laughed. "Good idea. Say, Jess, I've got something in my briefcase I wanted to show everyone. Could you go get it?"

"Sure," Jessica said, slipping out of her chair and going to the door.

"Aren't you forgetting something?" Mrs. Wakefield asked.

Jessica turned around. Her mother had one hand on the "baby."

"You can't leave a baby just sitting on a table when you leave the room," Mrs. Wakefield pointed out.

"Oops," Jessica said, running back. She

29

picked it up and set it down next to Elizabeth. "Will you baby-sit for me?"

"Oh, brother! I knew I'd end up doing the work," Elizabeth groaned. "I'll be baby-sitting this bag of beans all week."

"Don't forget, Liz," Jessica said as she hurried to the door. "You get to go to the water-slide park, too!"

"I guess you're pretty confident you can do it," Mrs. Wakefield said.

Jessica made a thumbs-up sign. "It'll be a snap."

CHAPTER 5

Baby-sitting

Jessica carefully carried her "baby" to school the next day. She placed it on her desk in their classroom and breathed a sigh of relief.

"Why are you carrying a bag of beans, Jessica?" Mrs. Otis asked. "Is it for show-and-tell?"

"It's a baby," Jessica explained.

Some of the kids standing nearby walked over to see what Jessica was talking about. "What do you mean, it's a baby?" Lila demanded.

"I made a bet with my mother that I

could take care of a baby for a week," Jessica said.

"What will you win?" Julie asked as she joined the group.

"A trip to the water-slide park," Elizabeth put in. "But if she loses, she has to wash our mother's car."

"But I'm not going to lose, because it's the easiest bet in the world," Jessica said confidently. She picked up the bag and held it out to Julie. "Want to hold my baby?"

Julie laughed. "Sure." She pretended to tickle the baby under the chin. "Gootchy-goo," she cooed.

The other girls all giggled, and Ellen began to talk baby talk to the bag of beans.

"Now Julie's got a baby," Ken teased. "You'll be safer holding a baby than trying to learn karate."

"That's the dumbest thing I ever heard," Elizabeth said. She shook her head at Ken.

"Didn't you hear Mr. Ogata? He said even a small person can beat a powerful enemy."

Ken just laughed and walked away.

"Girls can do anything they want, right, Mrs. Otis?" Elizabeth asked.

"Absolutely," Mrs. Otis said firmly as she began writing the class schedule on the blackboard. "There are plenty of girls who earn a black belt in karate."

"That's true," Julie said. "I've seen lots of girls at the karate tournaments. And I've seen lots of them win!" she added loudly, looking at Ken.

"Let's practice those blocks during recess," Elizabeth suggested to Julie.

"Good idea," Julie agreed. She looked down at the bag of beans she was carrying. "Where's Jessica?"

Elizabeth glanced around. Jessica was talking to Lila and Ellen and putting her homework away in her desk.

"Jess!" Elizabeth called.

Jessica looked around, and Julie held out the baby. "Oh, I forgot!" Jessica said, giggling. She came back and took the baby from Julie.

"What are you going to do with it during gym class?" Julie asked.

"Good question," Elizabeth said.

Jessica smiled. She didn't look at all worried. "I'll think of something," she said, and carried the baby back to her desk.

Elizabeth and Julie shared a doubtful look. "She almost left it on the bus this morning," Elizabeth told Julie.

"She really thinks carrying that around all week is going to be easy?" Julie asked, arching her eyebrows in disbelief.

Elizabeth sighed. "I have a funny feeling I won't be going to the water-slide park on Saturday."

CHAPTER 6

A Trip to the Library

After attendance and the Pledge of Allegiance, the class got ready to go to the library.

"Don't forget to return the books you took out last week," Mrs. Otis reminded them. "Line up single file, and please keep the noise to a minimum in the hallway!"

Jessica didn't have books to return, so she picked up her baby and stood in line. "See," she told Elizabeth. "I didn't forget it, and I bet you thought I would."

Elizabeth shrugged. "I'm glad you didn't. I want you to win."

"And I will," Jessica said. She switched the baby from one arm to the other.

"Getting tired?" Elizabeth asked.

Jessica shook her head quickly. "Oh, no," she fibbed. "It's not heavy at all."

Lila patted Jessica's baby on the head. "Want to do double-Dutch jump rope during recess?" she asked Jessica.

"Definitely," Jessica said.

The class trooped out of the room and down the corridor to the school library. When they arrived, Mr. Pratt, the librarian, told them they could browse for fifteen minutes.

"And be sure to check out what we have on the new-books shelf," he added.

Jessica switched her baby from her left arm back to her right arm. The bag of beans had felt light at first, but it seemed to get heavier all the time. With the baby in her arm, she went to browse in the section of new books. There was a colorful, glossy book on ballet, but it was large and awkward. She couldn't pull it out from the shelf with just one hand.

"Can you hold my baby for a minute?" she asked Ellen.

"I can't," Ellen said, pulling a book off the shelf.

"Can you?" Jessica asked Sandy Ferris.

Sandy had her arms full of books. She gave Jessica a startled look. "I don't have three hands!"

Frowning, Jessica looked around for someone who could baby-sit. Everyone was busy taking books off the shelves and checking them out. With a glance behind her to see if anyone was watching, she put the baby on the top of the bookcase, out of the way. Jessica gave a sigh of relief and reached out to take the ballet book from the shelf.

"Jessica!"

Jessica spun around. "What?"

Mrs. Otis was pointing to the top of the bookcase. "What are you doing, putting a baby up high like that? That's terribly dangerous!"

Everyone laughed, and Jessica felt her cheeks turn pink. "Oh, all right," she muttered, putting the book back and taking down the baby.

Mrs. Otis gave Jessica a friendly smile. "I'm sorry if I embarrassed you, but you do want to live up to your side of the bet, don't you?"

"Yes," Jessica said, holding the baby in both arms. "But I can't take out books if I have to carry this."

"Maybe taking care of a baby is not as easy as you thought," Mrs. Otis said.

Sulking, Jessica went to a chair and sat down. If she couldn't carry any books, she

couldn't check out any books. And if she couldn't check out any books, there was no point in looking. Charlie, who was standing nearby, looked at her "baby" and began to laugh. Jessica glared at him.

Julie Porter was examining the sports section and took down a book. "Hey, this is a whole manual of karate," she exclaimed.

Charlie reached over and snatched the book out of Julie's hands. "You don't need this, pipsqueak. I'll take it."

"Hey, no fair!" Jessica spoke up loudly.

"I had it first," Julie said in a firm voice.

"Why don't you make me give it back?" Charlie taunted.

"Go on, Julie," Jessica said.

But Julie shook her head. "*Sensei* said we should walk away from fights. That's what I'm going to do."

40

"Good excuse." Charlie laughed. "You couldn't make me give it back if you tried."

Jessica was surprised to see how serious Julie looked.

"That's not the karate way, Charlie. I think you need that book more than I do," Julie said. Then she turned and walked away.

CHAPTER 7

Practice Makes Perfect

"*Banzai!*" Kisho jumped off the end of the slide, chopping an imaginary enemy with the side of his hand.

"*Banzai!*" Todd yelled. They were running and slashing the air with their hands, turning and kicking wildly.

"They're just making it up," Elizabeth said to Jessica. "I don't think they listened to Mr. Ogata at all."

Jessica was holding her bag of beans. "They just want to do what they see in the movies, instead of practicing," she agreed.

"Ready to play double Dutch?" Lila asked, running over to Jessica. Jessica nodded so hard that her ponytail bounced.

"What are you going to do with your baby?" Elizabeth asked.

Jessica looked around the playground. "I'll get someone to hold it," she said. "Hey, Lois!"

"Yes?" Lois Waller walked over. Her cardigan sweater was buttoned wrong.

"I bet you're a really good baby-sitter," Jessica said in a sweet voice. "Want to watch my baby for a few minutes? I'll be right back."

Lois beamed. "Sure, Jessica." As Jessica and Lila ran off, Lois sat down on a bench to mind the baby.

"Make sure Jessica takes it back," Elizabeth said in a warning voice. "She'll make you hold it for all of recess unless you watch out."

"I don't mind," Lois said cheerfully.

For a moment Elizabeth watched the boys acting out their karate adventures. Then she noticed Julie standing by herself, practicing the blocks Mr. Ogata had taught them. Elizabeth ran over to join her. "Hi, Julie."

Julie raised her right arm in a block, her left fist by her side. Then she quickly switched arms. Then she switched them again.

"I'm trying to get this perfect," Julie explained. "It's so much harder than it looks! I want to make it exactly the same each time."

"Doesn't it get boring?" Elizabeth asked, watching as Julie continued practicing.

"Not really," Julie said. "Besides, that's what the *sensei* told us to do. I want to show him I can be disciplined."

Elizabeth stood beside Julie and began practicing the arm blocks, too. She closed her eyes and concentrated on moving her arms at the same speed. Each time she switched arms, she tried to end up in the same position.

"It is hard," she agreed.

"Try it really slow," Julie suggested. "That way you can be sure it's controlled."

Elizabeth and Julie practiced for several minutes, hardly even speaking. Both of them were concentrating on perfecting the movements. Elizabeth's arms began to get tired, but she kept working.

Then Charlie, Ken, and Kisho ran by. They stopped when they saw Julie and Elizabeth.

"Teacher's pets!" Charlie teased. "Look at me, I'm practicing!" He made an exaggerated imitation of the girls, squeezing his eyes shut tight.

"Very funny, Charlie," Elizabeth said.

"Try to attack me, Julie," Kisho said. "Come on, I dare you!" He jumped to the side, swinging his arms.

"I'm not going to do fake karate," Julie said, looking squarely at Kisho. "I'm going to do it right."

"Dumb girls," Kisho said, waving at Ken and Charlie. "Come on. Let's get out of here."

"I don't care how long it takes or how dumb I look," Julie said to Elizabeth. "I'm going to practice until I can do it perfectly."

Just then Jessica ran by on her way to the slide.

"Jess! Where's your baby?" Elizabeth called out.

"Lois has it," Jessica answered.

Elizabeth pointed to Lois, who was on the swings. Jessica's mouth dropped open.

"Lois," she yelled. "Where's the baby?"

"I got bored, so I gave it to Ellen," Lois

answered, swinging back and forth.

Jessica turned around and around, searching the playground for Ellen. "Oh, no," she whispered to Elizabeth. "Ellen is playing tag!"

Elizabeth and Jessica stared at each other in dismay. "We have to find it!" Jessica wailed.

"*We?*" Elizabeth repeated. "Mom said it was your responsibility."

"Just help me find it," Jessica said impatiently, tugging on Elizabeth's hand. "Come on, we'll—Oh! There it is!"

She dashed over to the jungle gym. The bag of beans was on the ground at the bottom of a ladder. Jessica scooped it up, brushed off the sand, and hugged it close. "Phew," she said as Elizabeth shook her head. "That was close."

CHAPTER 8

Star of the Class

Before gym the next day, Jessica showed her baby to the karate instructor. "Is it okay if I leave it on the floor near me? I have to watch it all the time," she explained.

Mr. Ogata smiled kindly. "Of course. It is very good to look out for others."

"Thanks." Jessica set the bag down carefully and stood beside Elizabeth.

"Now, how many of you have been practicing the blocks I taught you?" Mr. Ogata asked the class.

Some of the students couldn't remember the proper way to do the blocks, and many of the boys tried to show off by doing it fast. But Julie and Elizabeth stood in the correct stance and carefully demonstrated the arm blocks for Mr. Ogata.

"Did you practice?" Jessica whispered to Lila.

"No way, who wants to practice?" Lila asked with a shrug.

Mr. Ogata clapped his hands. "Now I will make new pairs, according to ability," he announced. "And then we will learn some kicking techniques."

Jessica held her breath as Mr. Ogata began separating buddies. "But we're always buddies!" she whispered to Elizabeth.

"I guess you should have practiced," Elizabeth replied.

"I couldn't with that dumb baby!" Jessica said.

Jessica watched glumly as Mr. Ogata paired Julie and Elizabeth together. Then she pouted as he told her to pair up with Lois.

"I knew I wouldn't be any good at this," Lois said, giving Jessica a smile.

"Now we will learn to kick," Mr. Ogata said, pacing slowly in front of the class. "I will need someone to help me demonstrate."

"Me! Me!" Ken shouted.

Kisho waved his hand in the air. "I'll help!"

Mr. Ogata stopped in front of Julie. "I will ask you to help me."

Bright-eyed with excitement, Julie walked to the center of the group with Mr. Ogata. He bent down on his hands and knees at her left side.

"Lift up your knee, and then kick over me, to the side," he told her.

50

Julie frowned in concentration, lifted her left leg, and kicked it straight out, over Mr. Ogata. She hopped a step to regain her balance, and then stood up straight again.

"Julie, that was a great kick!" Elizabeth exclaimed.

Mr. Ogata bowed to Julie. "Thank you," he said.

Jessica noticed that Todd, Kisho, and Charlie all looked jealous.

"Now I want you to practice that technique with your partners," the *sensei* said. "One person on the floor, and the other person kicking over their partner's back."

"What if my partner kicks me by mistake?" Lila asked in a loud voice, glancing at Ellen.

"Maybe it won't be a mistake," Todd said.

Mr. Ogata clapped his hands. "Remember discipline and self-control! If you are concentrating, there will be no mistakes."

Jessica looked doubtfully at Lois. "Want me to kick first?" she asked. "I promise not to kick you."

"Well . . ." Lois shrugged and glanced around the gym.

Most of the pairs were already practicing. Jessica took a step backward to get ready and almost stepped on her bag of beans.

"Look out!" Lois warned.

"Yikes!" Jessica looked down at her "baby." "I bet I can kick over that, no problem," she said.

She lifted her knee and kicked high over the small bag, then giggled. "See? Now let me try kicking over you."

"Okay," Lois said, kneeling on the floor. "But be careful!"

Just then there was a loud yell. Ken jumped up from the floor, rubbing his shoulder and glaring at Kisho. Kisho looked very embarrassed.

"Sorry," Kisho muttered.

Jessica gave Lois a reassuring smile. "Don't worry. I might not be very good, but at least I can do better than Kisho can!"

CHAPTER 9

Julie the Black Belt

During recess on Thursday, Elizabeth and Julie worked on the blocks and kicks they had learned, although no one else bothered to practice. Jessica lost her baby twice during school, and on Thursday night she left it outside in the backyard. Elizabeth found it and brought it inside before Mrs. Wakefield noticed.

"That baby is pretty dirty," Elizabeth said to Jessica Friday morning at the bus stop.

Jessica wrinkled her nose. "Do you think I should have given it a bath?"

"No." Elizabeth giggled. "The beans would get soaked."

"Even if it is dirty, today's Friday," Jessica said happily. "I just have one more day."

"And then water-slide park, here we come!" Elizabeth said.

When it was time for their last karate lesson, Mrs. Otis's class filed noisily into the gymnasium. Mr. Ogata was nowhere in sight, and the students stood in groups talking and waiting for class to begin.

"I bet Mr. Ogata asks Julie to come to his karate school," Elizabeth said to her sister. "She's definitely the best in class."

"You were good, too," Jessica said, shifting her baby from one arm to the other.

Elizabeth smiled. "Thanks."

Julie knelt down to open up the blue book bag she was carrying and took out a white jacket and green scarf. "Look," she said, holding it up to show Elizabeth. "It's not a real karate uniform, but it looks like one."

"Hey, look at Julie!" Charlie taunted from across the gym. "She thinks she's a real karate fighter."

"She's better than you are," Elizabeth said.

Julie didn't say anything. She put on the jacket and tied the scarf around her waist.

"Come on, Julie," Charlie continued. "See if you can kick me! Can you kick that high, or are you too small?"

"I'm not too small," Julie said in a quiet voice. "But I won't kick you."

Charlie grinned. "That's because you know you can't."

"Stop teasing me, Charlie. I mean it!" Julie said, her voice rising.

"Stop teasing me!" Charlie mocked her. "There's no way you could kick as high as my chest. You're too shrimpy and too weak to be any good at karate—*whoa!*"

Julie took a running jump and kicked out and up toward Charlie's chest. He sprang backward into Kisho, who went stumbling into Ellen, who screamed and bumped against Jessica, who fell forward. The baby went sailing out of her arms and landed on the floor, where it split open. Beans scattered in every direction.

"My baby!" Jessica screamed.

There was a shocked silence. Elizabeth gaped at Julie, who was standing still with both hands over her mouth. In the sudden stillness Mr. Ogata walked into the center of the group.

"This is what comes of anger," the *sensei* said in his quiet voice. He shook his head sadly. "I told you all that fighting in anger means someone will be hurt."

"But it's just a bag of beans," Todd spoke up nervously.

Jessica turned and stared hard at Todd. Elizabeth felt terrible for Jessica, and for Julie. Julie's face was bright red with embarrassment.

"I'm sorry, sensei," Julie whispered tearfully. "I meant to be disciplined, but I was so angry."

"She nearly kicked me right in the chest," Charlie complained loudly. "If I hadn't jumped out of the way—"

"If you had not picked the fight, this would not have happened," Mr. Ogata said to Charlie. "You are as much to blame."

Everyone was too embarrassed to speak. Then Jessica broke the silence. "Someone has to help me pick up all those beans!"

Lila giggled. "Now you'll have to wash your mother's car," she reminded Jessica.

Andy Franklin got a broom from Mr. Cutler's office. As soon as the beans were all swept up, Mr. Ogata gave the class their last karate lesson. Elizabeth and Julie were paired up again, and Elizabeth noticed that Julie worked harder than ever to make up for her mistake. While they practiced a new technique, Mr. Ogata stopped to speak to them.

"I hope you will never forget this most important lesson," Mr. Ogata said to Julie.

"I won't," Julie promised. "Not as long as I live."

The teacher smiled. "Maybe it's a good thing you learned it so soon, because it will make you better at karate. I believe you have the discipline to earn a black belt."

"Wow," Elizabeth gasped, staring at Julie.

The boys standing nearby stopped and gaped at Julie, too. "Did you hear that?" Todd said in astonishment. "A black belt!"

Elizabeth turned to Julie and they gave each other a high five.

CHAPTER 10

Cheating

"It's not my fault the baby got broken," Jessica complained as she stepped off the school bus that afternoon. "I was pushed."

"I know," Elizabeth said sympathetically. They walked up the sidewalk to their house. "It doesn't seem fair."

Jessica paused in front of the door and looked at Elizabeth with a hopeful expression on her face. "We could make a new one."

"Jessica! That would be cheating!" Elizabeth shook her head and reached for the door. "Besides, Mom would know. She always knows."

"No, wait!" Jessica said. "Please, Liz! There's no way Mom will know the difference, and it isn't really cheating—you saw what happened! You said yourself it doesn't seem fair. Besides, you get to go to the water-slide park, too," she added.

Elizabeth hesitated. "Well . . ."

"Pretty please?" Jessica asked again. She could tell Elizabeth was on her side.

"Okay." Elizabeth opened the door. "But we have to do it fast, or else Mom will find us."

"It'll just take a second," Jessica whispered, leading the way to the kitchen.

They tiptoed through the house as quietly as two mice. Jessica slowly slid open the drawer in the kitchen where the plastic bags were stored. She carefully took one out.

"I'll get the beans," Elizabeth whispered.

There was a footstep overhead, and the twins froze. Jessica felt her heart pounding. "Hurry!" she cried.

Quickly, they filled the plastic bag with dried beans and wrapped it up tightly with masking tape. In her best printing Elizabeth wrote "Jessica's Baby" on the outside of the bag. "I think it looks the same," Elizabeth said.

"It's perfect," Jessica agreed, glancing at the door. "Come on."

They ran out into the hallway. "Mom?" Jessica called. "We're home!"

Mrs. Wakefield came down the staircase, holding the toolbox. "Hi! I was just fixing that leaky pipe in the bathroom," she said with a smile. "How was school?"

"Good, Mom," Jessica said. "And look, here's the baby. I won the bet."

"Well, look at that," their mother said in surprise. "It's so clean. You've been taking extra good care of it, I see."

Jessica held her hand behind her back and crossed her fingers. "Yes," she said, without meeting Mrs. Wakefield's eyes. Inside her sneakers she crossed her toes.

"Here, let me take a look," their mother said. She held out her hands for the bag of beans.

"Why?" Jessica asked, beginning to grow nervous.

Mrs. Wakefield gave the twins a mysterious smile. "Just a little precaution I took," she said.

Jessica and Elizabeth looked at each other in alarm and followed their mother into the kitchen. Mrs. Wakefield took a pair of scissors and cut open the bag, spilling the beans onto a platter. She stirred the beans with one finger, frown-

ing thoughtfully. Jessica held her breath.

At last Mrs. Wakefield chuckled. "I thought this might happen," she said, looking at Jessica. "This isn't the same baby I made for you, is it?"

Gulping hard, Jessica shook her head. "How did you know?"

"I put one piece of macaroni in the bag when I made it," Mrs. Wakefield explained with a laugh. "And I don't see any macaroni here."

Elizabeth began to giggle. "Well, the baby had a terrible accident in karate class," she said. "It really wasn't Jessica's fault."

Mrs. Wakefield crossed her arms. "A deal is a deal. It wasn't so easy to take care of, was it?"

"No," Jessica admitted. "It wasn't."

"The boys were wrong about two things," Elizabeth said. "Girls *can* be really great at karate, and they aren't always good at taking care of babies!"

"Do I still have to wash your car?" Jessica asked.

Mrs. Wakefield smiled. "Yes. But all things considered, I think you've earned a trip to the water-slide park, too."

"Yippee!" Jessica yelled.

The telephone rang, and Elizabeth ran to answer it. She smiled. "Hi, Julie," she said. "Wow, that's great!"

"What happened?" Jessica asked when Elizabeth hung up the phone.

"Julie's parents are letting her sign up for Mr. Ogata's karate school," Elizabeth said. "And she says we'll be invited to her first karate match."

Jessica grinned at their mother. "That'll be fun. But I think I'll leave the baby at home."

*   *   *

On Monday morning all the girls gathered around the hamsters' cages to hear about Julie's first karate lesson. Jessica even noticed a few of the boys hanging around to listen. When Julie demonstrated a new kick she had learned, Ken and Todd both looked impressed.

"You're a real karate expert, Julie," Kisho said admiringly. "Do you think Mr. Ogata would let me sign up for some lessons?"

"I'm sick of karate," Lila said. "Why can't we talk about something more exciting for a change?"

"Like what?" asked Ellen.

"Like Halloween! It's only two weeks away," Lila said with a smug smile. "It's going to be the best Halloween ever, because I'm going to have the best costume ever!"

"Mrs. Otis says there's going to be a

great prize for the most imaginative costume," Lois said.

"If there's a prize, *I'm* going to win it,"
Jessica announced, looking at Lila. "My
costume will be the best of all!"

**Will Jessica win the big Halloween
contest? Find out in Sweet Valley
Kids #53, *The Magic Puppets*.**

SIGN UP FOR THE SWEET VALLEY HIGH® FAN CLUB!

Hey, girls! Get all the gossip on Sweet Valley High's® most popular teenagers when you join our fantastic Fan Club! As a member, you'll get all of this really cool stuff:

- Membership Card with your own personal Fan Club ID number
- A Sweet Valley High® Secret Treasure Box
- Sweet Valley High® Stationery
- Official Fan Club Pencil (for secret note writing!)
- Three Bookmarks
- A "Members Only" Door Hanger
- Two Skeins of J. & P. Coats® Embroidery Floss with flower barrette instruction leaflet
- Two editions of *The Oracle* newsletter
- Plus exclusive Sweet Valley High® product offers, special savings, contests, and much more!

Be the first to find out what Jessica & Elizabeth Wakefield are up to by joining the Sweet Valley High® Fan Club for the one-year membership fee of only $6.25 each for U.S. residents, $8.25 for Canadian residents (U.S. currency). Includes shipping & handling.

Send a check or money order (do not send cash) made payable to "Sweet Valley High® Fan Club" along with this form to:

SWEET VALLEY HIGH® FAN CLUB, BOX 3919-B, SCHAUMBURG, IL 60168-3919

NAME_____
           (Please print clearly)

ADDRESS_____

CITY_____ STATE _____ ZIP_____
                                                    (Required)

AGE_____ BIRTHDAY_____ /_____ /_____

SWEET VALLEY KIDS

Jessica and Elizabeth have had lots of adventures in *Sweet Valley High* and *Sweet Valley Twins*...now read about the twins at age seven! You'll love all the fun that comes with being seven—birthday parties, playing dress-up, class projects, putting on puppet shows and plays, losing a tooth, setting up lemonade stands, caring for animals and much more! It's all part of SWEET VALLEY KIDS. Read them all!

☐	JESSICA AND THE SPELLING-BEE SURPRISE #21	15917-8	$2.99
☐	SWEET VALLEY SLUMBER PARTY #22	15934-8	$2.99
☐	LILA'S HAUNTED HOUSE PARTY # 23	15919-4	$2.99
☐	COUSIN KELLY'S FAMILY SECRET # 24	15920-8	$2.99
☐	LEFT-OUT ELIZABETH # 25	15921-6	$2.99
☐	JESSICA'S SNOBBY CLUB # 26	15922-4	$2.99
☐	THE SWEET VALLEY CLEANUP TEAM # 27	15923-2	$2.99
☐	ELIZABETH MEETS HER HERO #28	15924-0	$2.99
☐	ANDY AND THE ALIEN # 29	15925-9	$2.99
☐	JESSICA'S UNBURIED TREASURE # 30	15926-7	$2.99
☐	ELIZABETH AND JESSICA RUN AWAY # 31	48004-9	$2.99
☐	LEFT BACK! #32	48005-7	$2.99
☐	CAROLINE'S HALLOWEEN SPELL # 33	48006-5	$2.99
☐	THE BEST THANKSGIVING EVER # 34	48007-3	$2.99
☐	ELIZABETH'S BROKEN ARM # 35	48009-X	$2.99
☐	ELIZABETH'S VIDEO FEVER # 36	48010-3	$2.99
☐	THE BIG RACE # 37	48011-1	$2.99
☐	GOODBYE, EVA? # 38	48012-X	$2.99
☐	ELLEN IS HOME ALONE # 39	48013-8	$2.99
☐	ROBIN IN THE MIDDLE #40	48014-6	$2.99
☐	THE MISSING TEA SET # 41	48015-4	$2.99
☐	JESSICA'S MONSTER NIGHTMARE # 42	48008-1	$2.99
☐	JESSICA GETS SPOOKED # 43	48094-4	$2.99
☐	THE TWINS BIG POW-WOW # 44	48098-7	$2.99
☐	ELIZABETH'S PIANO LESSONS # 45	48102-9	$2.99